EXPLORERS

Written by David Lloyd
Illustrated by Jane Johnson

WALKER BOOKS
LONDON

Mary, William and Lucy were looking at a book about jungles.

'Let's pretend to be explorers,' William said.

'The whole house can be the jungle,' Mary said.

'I don't like jungle games,' Lucy said.

'The jungle is very shadowy and hot,' William said.
'We're looking for rare animals,' Mary said.

'I want to go in the garden,' Lucy said.

'Listen! Did you hear that?' William whispered.
'It was a barking monkey,' Mary said.

'It wasn't, it was next door's dog,' said Lucy.

William and Mary went deeper into the jungle,
taking Lucy with them.

'Hold my hand here, Lucy,'
Mary said. 'There may
be snakes.'

'You're just pretending,'
said Lucy.

Lucy lay down on the jungle
floor and wouldn't move.
'We'll have to leave you,'
William said.

'I know you're pretending,' said Lucy.

Jungle eyes were watching.
Jungle beasts were waiting.

Lucy was alone. A tiger roared.

Lucy got up and ran out of the jungle door.

William and Mary came back. Lucy had gone.

'The beasts must have taken her,' William said.
'Poor Lucy,' Mary said. 'Perhaps there's still
time to save her.'

William and Mary found Lucy in the garden.
She was happy now and holding something.
'What have you got, Lucy?' Mary asked.

'A snail,' said Lucy, 'and I'm not pretending.'